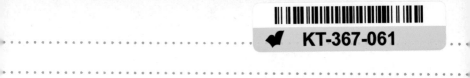

I Am the Way I Am

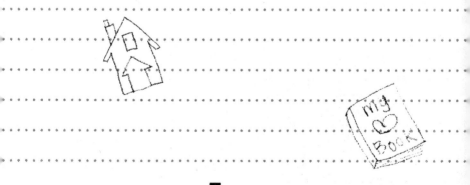

Lizzie and Tilly were twins. Though they looked the same, it was easy to tell who was who by the way they were.

Lizzie was tidy. She brushed her hair often. She fussed about what to wear.

Tilly didn't care what her hair looked like. She wore the same clothes for as long as she could.

7

Lizzie liked
making lists.
Tilly liked
hiding in
secret places.

The girls didn't mind being
different, but one thing made them
both *really* cross. Their bedroom.

Lizzie kept her side of the room
neat and organized. She was proud
of her bed. She smoothed the sheets and
straightened the duvet. In the middle of
three pretty pillows sat one large doll.
When Lizzie read, she sat
in a chair.

Nothing on Tilly's side of the room was neat. Her teddies lay higgledy-piggledy. She *sort of* made her bed. She loved jumping on it to try and touch the ceiling.

When Mum looked in, she would say, "Tilly! You're louder than a bus-load of monkeys!"

Then Lizzie would sigh. "She's so noisy, it's hard to read."

"I am the way I am!" Tilly would bounce even higher, "I don't want to change."

It was a rainy
Saturday
morning.
"Nothing
to do,"
grizzled Tilly.

Mum grinned
and pointed
to their room
upstairs. "Oh
yes there is…"

Lizzie began by tidying her books. "Small books at this end of the shelf," she said. "Big books at that end."

Tilly stacked her books on the floor. Just then, one stack fell onto another.

"See what happens when you don't take care?" Lizzie grumbled.

Tilly flopped on her bed.
She read while Lizzie stacked
Tilly's books into sizes.

Dad looked in. "Tilly!
Got your sister working
for you again?"

Lizzie sighed.
"She's *so* messy, Dad!"
"Better than being fussy," Tilly mumbled into her book.

Lizzie's socks were rolled into pairs. Her shoes formed a straight line. On her drawers and shelves were labels saying what went where.

Tilly might have been messy, but she knew where important things were. Like Bunji and Delilah.

"Let's make our pencils into a long rainbow!" Lizzie clapped.

"What's that noise?" Tilly rushed away. Laughing, she swung on the swing with her head upside down. Then she climbed the old tree to see far away.

"*I am the way I am,*
that's why I'm me!" she sang.
She didn't know, but Lizzie
was singing the same song.

17

"We look the same," said Tilly that night in bed. (She liked thinking before sleeping.) "So why are we different?"

"Because you eat green jellybeans," Lizzie mumbled, half-asleep.

Tilly stared, thinking in the dark. It was true! Lizzie didn't like anything green. *If I didn't eat green jellybeans, would I be more like Lizzie? If Lizzie liked green, would she be more like me?*

Tilly dreamt she was swimming in green goo. Lizzie was swimming too but she looked like a frog. Lizzie dreamt they were playing hopscotch. Every pebble she threw refused to land and Tilly jumped all over the place. Then she hopped backwards until she disappeared.

The twins woke at the same time.
They looked the same first thing.
"I had a strange dream about you,"
they said together.

The girls dressed for school
and brushed their hair
and looked the same.

They enjoyed making
their lunch. Lizzie loved jam
sandwiches, Tilly liked ham.

Lizzie had a yellow lunchbox,
Tilly had green.

"What do you girls do at
lunchtime?" asked Dad.

"Play hopscotch!" shouted Tilly.

After her dream, Lizzie thought it best not to play today.

Tilly's hair was already fluffing up. Her shoelaces were already undone.

"Surprise!" said Mum. "Look what Grandma left behind. Jellybeans to share after lunch!"

Tilly looked sideways at Lizzie. Did her sister just croak…?

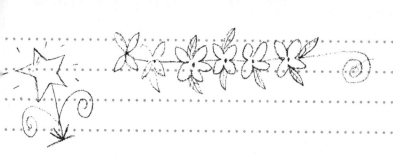

The Same Game

It was a grey, going-nowhere kind of day. Grandma and Mum chatted. Tilly was reading. Lizzie was bored.

"Let's make a list," Lizzie said, "about how we're different. Or – how we're the same."

Tilly didn't look up. "Why?"

"Because," said Lizzie, "then we'll know what to say when people ask what it's like being twins."

27

"That's not the real reason." Tilly
turned a page.

"What is it, then?"

"You just love making lists."

Tilly wanted to read,
but Lizzie needed help.
Tilly thought for a bit,
then smiled.

"The list has to be Things We Both Like Doing," she said. Then added, "At the Table." *This will be the world's shortest list,* she grinned to herself. *Because there are only two things worth doing at a table!*

Lizzie took a while to find the right paper and right pencil.

The pencil needed sharpening. Tilly got quite a bit of reading done.

Lizzie always washed hands before starting, so she wouldn't smudge the paper. She used her ruler to make her coloured pencils perfectly straight. She spent more time preparing than drawing.

"First I'll
write the
heading,"
she said,
and smoothed
the paper.

Tilly read
on while Lizzie
solved the

problem of which colours to use.

"Number 1," Lizzie called.

"Drawing," said Tilly.

"Yes. We both
like drawing."

Tilly went on
reading.

"Drawing patterns is best," Lizzie hummed. "Especially stars."

Tilly watched her sister draw a large star. "Stars are too easy. Drawing animals is better. Especially donkeys!"

Lizzie waved her rubber. "Should 'Drawing' be on the list, then? It has to be what we like doing the same."

Tilly thought carefully. "Yes. We both like drawing. It doesn't matter what we draw."

Lizzie was glad
she didn't have to
rub out her star.
"Number 2?"

"Eating."
Tilly was ready
to read again.
"But we
don't like eating
the same things,"
groaned Lizzie.

"I hate green
beans and you
love them. I love
chicken soup
and you hate it."

Tilly had the answer. "We both love spaghetti."

She always made a mess with her spaghetti. Yum! *Sluuurp! Ping!* Sauce on chin.

Lizzie always twirled her fork round and round slowly, one strand at a time. No sauce smears on her!

Lizzie wrote "Eating", then went off to ask Mum how to spell spaghetti.

Tilly relaxed, sure the list was now finished.

Lizzie wrote number 3. "I could put 'Jigsaws'." She frowned at her sister. "But you don't play properly. You force pieces to fit."

"Not forcing, *testing*."

"Force."

"Don't."

"Do so!"

"DO NOT!"

"Girls!" called Mum. "No fighting!"

"We aren't!" shouted Tilly.

"Are," whispered Lizzie.

"Not," hissed Tilly.

"What else do we like doing at the table?"

"Reading," Tilly growled.

"But I read in my special chair."

"I read on my bed. But we *could* both read at the table."

"But I don't."

"But you could."

"But I don't!"

"You could TRY!"

"Girls!" Mum shouted.

"Why did it have to be things at the table?" hissed Lizzie.

"Because." The world's shortest list was taking *for ever*.

Things we both like doing at The Table

1. Drawing
2. Eating Spaghetti
3. ~~Jigsaws~~
~~Reading~~

X

"What are you two up to?" Grandma peered over Lizzie's shoulder.

"A list of things we both like doing at the table. Tilly's stupid idea!"

Grandma winked. "Put down 'Fighting'."

The twins shrugged. "Yes," they mumbled. "Fighting."

Lizzie thought this
list was the worst she'd
ever made.

"How disappointing,"
Grandma tutted.
"You've forgotten what
we all love doing at
my table!"

The girls glared. Then laughed.
Lizzie happily wrote number 4
before Grandma returned.

"Clear the decks!" Grandma pulled old magazines from her workbag.

"Scrapbooks, glue, scissors. Glitter, sticker-stars."

Mum joined in.
They sat
at the table
for hours.

Later Lizzie wrote:

     5. Laughing.

     6. Talking.

     7. Being Happy.

Things we both like doing at The Table

1. Drawing
2. Eating Spaghetti
3. ~~Jigsaws~~
~~Reading~~ Fighting
4. Sticking
5. laughing
6. Talking
7. Being Happy

Just Not You

45

The day started badly. Tilly got out
of bed first and slid on a book she'd
dropped the night before. That made
her bang into a drawer she'd left open
before getting into bed. The little table
tilted, making Tilly's shell collection
fall on Lizzie's bed.

"I'm sick of you messing our room!" Lizzie whopped Tilly with her pillow.

"I'm sick of you fussing all the time!" Tilly bopped back.

"Mum and Dad know
I'm better than you!"
Lizzie swung.

Tilly's face went red.
"Don't care!"

"Slob!" Lizzie made
Tilly fall backwards.

"At least I'm not boring, like you!"
Tilly ran from the room.
She was crying.

Lizzie was
so angry,
she kicked
Tilly's pile
of books.

She jumped
all over
Tilly's bed.

She threw
her sister's
shoes out of
the window.

After a while,
Lizzie was sad
that she'd said
such horrible
things.

"Mum, have you seen Tilly?"

Mum was bringing in the washing.

"No, dear. Would you like to help sort these clothes?" Lizzie usually loved helping, but not this time.

"Tilly!" She
searched the garden.
Next door's dog
barked. But no
sound from her sister.
She found Dad
in his shed.

"No, I haven't seen Tilly."
He stopped hammering.
"But I've just the job for
you. Can you sort these
nails into sizes?"

But Lizzie was already running to the playground across the road. She crawled under bushes. She looked under bridges. She sploshed in puddles and tripped over tree roots. Had Tilly run away for ever? It was all her fault! Lizzie ran home crying. Mum and Dad would be *so* angry. What a terrible mess! Oh, where was Tilly?

Tilly was next door visiting
Mrs Labelle. Mrs Labelle's house
wasn't over-tidy or over-messy.

Tilly told her about the fight.

Mrs Labelle wanted to cheer Tilly up.

"In my house, Mr Labelle is the tidy one. I hate cleaning."

"Do you fight?" Tilly sniffed.

"Sometimes."

"Do you run away?"

"Sometimes, but not far. Then I cook a nice dinner. And Mr Labelle washes the dishes."

Tilly wiped her eyes. She still felt unhappy. Did Mum and Dad really love Lizzie more?

56

Mrs Labelle
gave her a hug.
"It's important
to be who we
are and to do
things we
like doing.

But sometimes it's all right to do things
that make other people happy too.
The fun thing is, when you are nice to
someone, you feel better. Surprises can
happen when you're kind – you'll see."

Through the window they saw Lizzie return from the playground. How dirty she was! How sorry she looked! Mum and Dad came running when they heard crying. They thought Lizzie was Tilly.

Dad cuddled her. "What's the matter, love? Lizzie's been looking for you."

Lizzie cried harder.

Mum smiled at the muddy footprints and gluggy shoes. "How I love my Tilly scruff-pot." She hugged Lizzie tightly.

Tilly grinned at Mrs Labelle. "Time to go home. This is a mess only I can fix."

Tilly walked up the path. Dad stared at Mum in surprise. "Do we have *two* Tillys?"

Lizzie ran to her sister. "I couldn't find you!" she cried.

Tilly grinned. "I'm good at hiding, remember?"

The twins
stared at their
messy room.
Lizzie
went red.

"What a fantastic mess!" Tilly
was impressed. She fluffed Lizzie's
hair. "Shall we tidy it together?"

Lizzie beamed in surprise. Tilly could
have been mean. She
tried smoothing
Tilly's hair.
Then they
both laughed.
"That's just
not you!"

"We'll tidy later." Lizzie
took Tilly's hand. "Show me
how to climb the old tree."

Tilly's eyes lit up. Mrs Labelle
was right about surprises. "When we
climb high enough, we'll see
the whole world!"